3/3

3v3ıytding

when you have already lived
all of your lives
and still, you continue
to find yourself
going and going and going
you are living

(34)

Three of 3v3rything

@toddymanners

for my beautiful
Soledad

totalllly for eternidad

belleza viaja
entre nosotros

BESOS! BESOS! BESOS!

♫ She is mi Esposa ♪
♪ She's my Soledad ♫
♩ Oh how I Love Her
How She Loves me back

Table of Contents

- - - - - - - - - = poem continues

___________ = poem complete

- - - - - - - - - = poem continues

___________ = poem complete

- - - - - - - - = poem continues

___________ = poem complete

- - - - - - - - = poem continues

___________ = poem complete

"Poem!" said the lightning, not thinking
to look both ways first "Poem!"
saying it again while bursting every
who-what-where thought
"Poem!" with serrated blades of
insistent electricity scissors
splitting pregnant storm clouds
opened with another "Poem!" bursts through

at
10,000 lumens

never to be caught by

"Poem!"...

...rumbling thunder.

a butterfly, who
you may fully disbelieve
is a butterfly,
is a butterfly.
the transition of being
one; being for one.

always listen to your wife
when she suggests that you take
a shower,
especially
if you're a writer
who,
like me, forgets.
it's likely that she has already
been
as patient
as she could possibly be, and
who knows,
the shower could be
        ... Hot... Perfect... Rain...
pouring from the ceiling,
not demanding
any prerequisite
tall-human-back-hunching
in order to receive
    the Melting of Everything.

thanks, Honey

AppleJacks naps

a ventriloquist has moved in,
throwing old man voices
into my throat anytime that I move
my bones and muscles into
familiar positions indicating
I'm on the verge
of standing up again, and
this has become terribly alarming to
my good dog AppleJacks, who can be
right in the middle of the deepest,
happiest dog naps,
chasing critters with non-committal
woof-yaps, telepathic dog dream
transmissions received, his legs
dream of cooperating with each other
just like mine do,
misbehaving like they'd forgotten
how to do the leg things they'd always
gotten to do
when my ventriloquist shows up.

throwing "oooph"s and "mmmph"s
at my tampered and toyed-with voice box;
just me, trying to stand up
having nothing to do with actually standing,
when sure enough,
here comes my understanding
fellow old man, AppleJacks,
running to me with his suddenly
wide awake
urgent legs at work
to check
on whether or not I'm still doing ok;
his tail wagging as soon as he sees
my eye contact
saying to him the answer is still yes;
his eyes looking back at mine with
dog sincerity, showing both
worry and relief, communicating
very clearly, his dog wishes saying
"please let that still-doing-ok thing
we've got going between you & me,
always be what humans promise is
garoof."

be cool

calibrating coolness
can't continue
finding its true north
chillax-point
without first
letting go of
      someone else's
               gotta-be

cooliosity.

Being, a man

about losing some friends, family,
and that childhood religion,
thought guaranteed believable
since the time of my crawling
towards hating what lives inside
of hiding who I am, after
admitting to being an unapologetic
pole smoker, so,
suddenly no more job or place
to live anywhere I couldn't;
moving to the big city to be
saturated with funeral burnout
by the age of thirty
seeing half of my community
killed by a virus that
"the good people of this country"
didn't give one single shit about,
from the president down,

because it was just fags;
turning their backs
or making jokes, instead.
surviving to fight
for the right to marry
the human being who I love
and who loves me with a
strength of heart I have
never known, living as though
it should have never been
anyone else's business... or
their right
to say "no" to
SOME, ANY or ALL of our LOVE
for either of us. Then,
seeing my brand new spouse
nearly lose her entire
military career after serving
sixteen honorable years;
being kicked to the curb
by full-of-shit politicians

--- 2 ----

who dodged ever serving
anyone but themselves,
criminally unjust,
only wanting to grim-reap
a handful of political capital;
my nearing-retirement
transgender wife nearly losing
her honorable years of service.
my wife...their fodder.
going to see a therapist
because of still...
not always being able...
to keep myself from crying
or thinking that I...
have lived way too damn long
through too much motherfucking
bullshit and loss
...continuing...
to have to fight to not look
at any of it
in order to continue living

all these years later, fighting
with automatic-happy
boxing gloves of
still being alive;

big strong man

saying "guess what...
all of this fucking mattered
and I have kept on breathing
for long enough
to write it all down, while
living every day; deeply true."

genuine, with gratitude,

forty years past the finish line.

blind choreography

what you believe
could be
what I believe and we would
have never known
that
about each other because
you and I are
two people to be kept locked
into being kept apart,
rather than standing right
next to each other, and,
even then, someone
who we don't even know, currently
makes tons of hate money,
making sure that
people like you and I
are kept in our own corners,
not talking with each other, at best,
friendship a maybe maybe not.

Bouquets I don't cut

Thank you, Charles Schulz,
    Mr. Rodgers and Jim Henson;
    Gilda Radner, Madelyn Kahn,
    John Belushi.
Thank you,
    Keith Haring, Vincent van Gogh.
Thank you, James Baldwin,
    Hillel Slovak, David Bowie,
    Freddie Mercury, Joe Strummer.
Thank you, Prince.
Thank you, great grandma
    and great grandpa
    Della Luella and James Leroy,
    Grandpa Bud and your
    boyfriend, John Midgeley.
Thank you, Mom and Dad,
    Drew, Kevin and Chris,
    my three forevers,

and Thank you, to every
Animal Family Member
who I have had the honor
and the privilege of joining here,
spending all of our beautiful life
together.
Thankyou, Halo'd J, my original Jesus,
my brother and hilarious pal,
carrying absolute love's
immensity, barefoot,
without losing
your heart's rhythmic stride.

Thank you because each one of you
has achieved greatness
in ways that has helped me to see
what I needed to find, guiding

the importance in life,
and

every one of you,
even with all of that
immortal greatness
kept intact,

died,

leaving
your greatness still alive,
with me at least
knowing that

I too will die;
dead dead dead while
    reaching for
    my favorite pen and one more
    piece of paper...

too late; my body
drawn up through
the breath of nourishing
Earth,
that vibration
finding greatness, as it always has,
always will;
you will die too,
no matter where all of your plans
land.
So what. Just
start with stopping
the bullshit, then

listen

to twelve different types of birds
    singing in the morning, and
        watching clouds move
                    faster than you.

cat litter

have you noticed that there are people
who treat other people
(eager, even)
the way that cats do fresh cat litter,
looking forward to making more mess
    the minute
        you've given
            some time for maintaining
            what had been there.
    The sound of cleaning the cat box
        catching their attention,
        clear from the other room, and,
    the very moment you are done,
            here they come,
    ready to release another load of
    judgmental poop and pee again.

shitty things

there used to be a television commercial
suggesting that you speculate
how many licks there were
before getting to the center of a sucker,
and I am left wondering about
how many shitty things
need to be said
about a person who you love
before you either
get to the chewy center or crack;
finding the courage to
call that bullshit out. Now,
complicate the question.
how many licks of shitty things is it
if the person
who is saying the shitty stuff
about you,
is also you;
losing track of your counting
while you get to the center,
or crack.

crackling chestnuts

Every family who celebrates,
   or once celebrated
Christmas has its own collection,
those beloved
"not-on-Christmas" greatest hits.
We all know the good one:
the Baby Jesus one, attached to
intending on behaving with
the unspoken level of respect
necessary to keep the Holy Babe
sleeping, but the unrest of the rest
of everything, churning,
becoming murky with uh-oh again.
Non-metaphorical shadows with
fingernails and teeth
made for ripping through traditions
presence, and thin, sugary skin,
licking

tasty mistletoe lips just foreplay
before libation's lamentations with
spiked drinks and hot, fresh,
homemade cookies in the oven "why
does it always have to be at
    Christmas." chugga-lugga that
misery, finding theatrics
irresistible during the holidays,
seeing and smelling
so many lit, scented candles,
carolers on vinyl, long play,
knowing their cues to enter this
stage right or risk being left
broken in half. That
tormented, human sound; heavy
footsteps and smashed ornaments
approach, their own advent
  calendars' tiny paper countdown
doors, all still closed … and those …
jingle bells thrown into the fire.

Our family's greatest hits,
popping like chestnuts again.

"Not on Christmas" is pure silliness
to insist every year, when of course,
it's Christmas again.
Unboxing dusty grudges
drug from the dusky basement
  for this...
to box each other with.

Lifelong family holiday traditions
singing together
  it's beginning to look a lot like
fuck
      Christmas. wishes kept quiet,
      that the holidays wouldn't
                      always
      get drop kicked by Santa.

denouement

thinking it couldn't have been much past
fourth grade when I learned
there was an ending
before the end;
one word in profile, appearing
like muerte
could not be more ready,
lying in its grave,
waiting for dirt
to start raining.

dismissed

you know what it feels like
if anyone has ever been
    dismissive
        of you even if
            they never found

the nuts to say
that's what they were doing
out loud, so if you ever
    find that
        I have been like that
                    with you,
you have my permission
to punch me squarely in the face
without asking,
        and move on.

Dissolving into one

in that moment, I knew
that I too
had captured the sun.
Seeing
my beautiful wife;
the glowing, familiar,
as if it had been born from the center
of one hand,
her arms extended
atop
supremely graceful curves
in symmetry
with Mother Ocean,
they swallow each other
in a primal dance of ecstatic beauty
connecting love, with something in me;
I yield my eyes.
Following her
generous currents through rip tides;
lifting
my feet from the ground, she is

holding my hand
with that warmth from the sun, and
together, we smile;
taking flight
again.

      —for my beautiful Soledad

      Catalina Island,
      and Venice Beach, 2024

Bikes
L♥VE
WH☺EVER
THE FUCK
Y♥U WANT

do you think
respect
needs to be automatic, a
one-sided given, for
someone else's strongly held
religious beliefs
that won't respect
your personhood,
your family, or
your love,
repeatedly speaking out about
your rights
          taking a back seat
            on good days,
              locked out on the rest
preached pulpit-to-sponge, and you,
given the generous option
of tossing
a shame-chasing shot back;
this delicious
blood of Jesus; just
sign our agreement to be pulled

along with us,
cluckine with conditional graces.
all of those salted tongues and
blood shooters
easing the bite
of not being able to speak out about
such and such
ruinous
bullshit, oh, hell no.
free from pinched lips and high-browed
worthiness; your measurements
are wearing falsies.
I already understand that
the best way to get to heaven
is to swallow hard
and die again
before inhaling the odors of putrified
righteousness grease, wafting
everywhere with sanctimonious airs
but,
...then again,
          and again again,
fucking just let them win

trapped inside of their tightening circles,

leaving you on your own, with

the freedom
to find everything
that mattered to begin with,
and that

is worth respecting.

111124

Equality +/-.

stating as fact that
anyone who has chosen
to have one or one hundred million
children
justifies
raising all of those
precious ones
the way that the parents choose
         (great! do it, but not)
through somehow curtailing
—any of the same rights—
—that all of us have—
      who
      the rearers
      just don't want
      their chosen bubble-children
      to know about,
meaning that our equal rights, somehow,
need to be halved or shushed,
like their choice to have kids
means the lesson is for

those of us who are
considered lesser, to ante up
and fork over our own rights.
the equivalent of being
on a speeding airline jet,
stuck in one seat while flying overnight,
over oceans,
swearing that you'll never fly again
   while listening
   to everyone's screaming children;
their innocent ears, popping,
not understanding
altitude changes and
   the most reasonable solution
   being
of course - to protect the children
by opening the emergency exit,
mid-flight,
and throwing everyone else out.

<hr>

ecstasy.

swimming didn't happen
the first time I was
thrown into a collection of letters & words.
at first
it was too alarming not feeling
my feet planted in the always
known gravity.
eyes ears nose mouth head now
shrouded and entered by letters
introducing equanimity
between my dog paddling feet as I find
the ecstasy of breaking
through my first
resurfacing; letters turned to
words sliding and gliding
from my temples

to my dripping chin
ignoring the hollered warnings
of lifeguards, thinking
incoming lightning storms had the power
to keep me
from going under.
Look at my arms!
shimmering with letters latched together
like moving boxcars.
Submerged.
Filling my lungs with breathing again.

91724

Emotional support kitten

Chuck,
doing what he does,
making every situation where he is
better,
just by being there.
His beautiful wife doesn't mind
my straight-man crush
bringing pure love through my pores
when I am near him and what is best
about that
is that
he is secure
in belonging within his own
man sexuality;
unthreatened by
having a gay guy saying
benign flirty things leaving his
masculinity totally unruffled.
Laughing with me about life and
all of its absurdities.
there for me in an instant

- - - - - - - - -

without question
for anything. Calling me brother and
showing me the truth of that sentiment
with his words and actions and
a true brother-hug,
awkward, at first, then learning it's
left chest to left chest
where your hearts are;
liberal with his love, without worrying
what anyone thinks about what
true masculinity
should be.
Chuck, free with being
truly present, with me.

eye level

from where I'm at

everything is

lining up,

however it does that,

for long enough

for remembering

to make a wish that this

frontwards or backwards

feeling

will stick.

fair warnings

if I am depressed
and you are a pizza,
or ice cream, sitting
all pretty
with a whole rhubarb pie,
you should probably
go hide somewhere
pretty quickly.

fam

you know who you are
 when you meet, and those
everyday-days don't need to be
anything special
in new ways each time because
when you're already swimming in
always-gonna-be,
even the sucky days, in some ways,
are gonna be great.
my fam; way more
one of finding
than born,
now never not always.
this version of best, is
the best of everything.

for Erin

<u>the</u>. <u>first</u>. <u>everlasting</u>

creativity came to life, first,
through convincing intensities;
those
insider-conversations whose purpose
        got built
        on what is already eternal.
giving its eyes away
    for unobstructed use to anyone
    who had forgotten how
to use their own visual telepathy;
we all go through this
blindness. Relying on decoding
tactile walls, not avoiding invisible
jump shadows, prisoners all,
lurking behind unlocked doors
thought of as survivalism
containing deadly seeds of
    ...self-destruction...waiting...
            to   remove
all of creativity's borrowed eyes,

Saying nothing but lies
   about you, and possibly even
your whole species, having nothing
to offer by nature of creativity,
when you are, at once,
                              opened:
   the eyes that you've got
      motherfucking evolving,
   exactly like nature said to;
wasting nothing.

flying by instruments

It would have been impossible
to find our way here, together,
through thick marine blanket layers
without running into trees or crashing
through asphalt.
Dozens of spinning dials,
counting up and down,
their long, comma-free numbers
knowing something about
getting here.
without seeing, exactly,
how to get here, knowing
the best horizontal there is.
Your satisfied head, resting on my chest,
my arm wrapped around your ample warmth,
restless my hand,
with the constant movement of
a cat's flickering tail, caressing perfect
pathways of curving
lily pad ribs bumping one-by-one beneath
the breath of my angled side-thumb

along your softness
aimed upward.
finding a blissline where
the palm of my hand
makes a decision
to quietly nudge my thumb
into collaboration
towards further nourishment;

        now gliding

  together
in alignment with friction,
somehow

finding ourselves
here;
gravity free.

4giveness

I can forgive
born family
and I can forgive friends
who abandoned me,
but
the only reason that I could ever think
of forgiving
the motherfucking mormon church is
because of the person who I became
after they ejected me
          with my nasty homosexuality...
otherwise, I would have never left; just
stuck, in what would have remained
an empty husk.
Now, outwardly free to begin
thinking:
how about those
who will likely never have reason
to find forgiveness
of me.

Say either
"I love you"
or "fuck you"
or whatever
you want,
but never say
the half-assed
"love you" to me,
ever.

those are your choices.

Galapagos

you don't SEE ME,
and I cannot
pay
for you to pay
(any)
attention;
this mere evolution
of
our shared SPECIES
has nothing to do
with your blinding
affliction's
isolation nightmare.

Ghost writer

You are not invisible to me.
I see you
because, like you,
I used to think in
invisibilizing terms
through the defining means of
so many others ahead of me,
but I just couldn't
(or didn't know how to)
keep on going with
not being seen.
I love you
and
I believe in you
writing things in your head
for other people to claim as
their own brave truths
about being gay or anything else
   that everyone says is bad,
with your
practiced words, while you remain,
for someone else's reasons,
invisible.
I see you and I hope that
one someday while
you are still alive
you are able to see
yourself
out loud about owning
your own words
with a broad smile that gets it
all neon-lit for every
still-invisibilized-self
to see,
the same way that I see you.

Chad didn't know that he mattered. In fact, because of everything that he'd ever heard, about people like him, from his friends, his family, his church, and from every peer who everyone else had decided mattered at school, he was convinced that he was the exact opposite of mattering to anyone. Keeping what was a scary-truth for him hidden, feeding the feeling of certainty that he mattered less when alive, than he would being dead; this… by the time he was fifteen.

Silently taking ubiquitous cues from so many people around him, he'd become convinced that talking with anyone about how he felt would only make everything worse, sealing within him a hatred for himself, that was miles deeper than any hole that anyone else could have ever dug for him; remaining trapped within his own deadly fears.

People love to hear and tell ghost stories, except for the ones involving ghosts who they know, who are still living with actual heartbeats among them. Nobody wants to think or talk too much about the sad stuff that lives in realtime; leaving it understood that there are no entry points for love or respect to merge with truthful conversations about what everyone agrees, without speaking, needs to be left alone, and unsaid…

To Chad, it appeared that there were only exits left, anyway. Worrying, well before dying, about any big sadness happening for those around him, whether he attempted to explain how sunken he'd been feeling, before he actually left, or waiting until after he'd intentionally sunk himself… into the warmth of the welcoming earth.

Either way, he couldn't leave those reasons or questions unanswered, deciding to become his own ghost writer; his wounded alphabet, letters carefully strung together into words left in knots to be untangled by another; spelling out his unexplainable breakdown, for whenever, whomever, or whatever came next. Ultimately, surprising himself with sentences that left him finding that there is still hope, even at the end, that his words would know how to go on living; saying:

"I promised myself that I'd give it another year, to see if anything would change. I kept that promise for nothing. Then, my promise and my plans reached forward to two years, and part-way into the third, just in case something or someone would give me reason to believe… that I would be seen… someday… without being judged, juried, and ejected by my peers… but that didn't work out either. So, with 17 years of too-old-for-this, I pushed through my own sparkling turnstile, into the universal-next-round where I remain unseen by any people who are still here; just like before. Although now, my invisibility has become irreversible, by my own hand. And while everyone is left wringing their hands, and furrowing their foreheads with confusion, I wish that someone, anyone, would have helped me to see that with the short time I'd had in life, as a teenage kid, those overly concentrated ratios, of range and perspective, had skewed into my thinking that what I could see, at that time in my life, was everything that I would ever see as true, about myself or anyone.

Like wading through waves of a concave body-length circus mirror, having only seventeen years worth of timeline to draw experience from, had warped my suspension-of-disbelief into thinking that what I could see at that moment was the way of everything; all of it truthful, all of it for forever. The scary ghost story being the one that made me believe I'd never matter, at least not in a respected, loving way, without changing everything about me that couldn't be changed; leaving me convinced this was the only way that I would ever feel; the truth, gone stuck upside-down.

This is where you come in. You… someone who still has a chance of leaving that funhouse hall-of-mirrors another way. I smashed head-first through my own warped reflection, and now, I see you looking at yours; believing that the twisted-soul-traps laid by others are somehow your only home too.

I think that this is the part of any ghost story where I'm supposed to yell "Boo!" with a thunderous, disembodied voice that no one ever seems prepared to hear unless it's at Halloween. Although, countless generations of self-enders before us, have long shared their voices, with warnings of what we had remained too afraid to hear, only this:

we didn't need to remain afraid
of finding our own way of being
two things at once;
both alive, and living.

I am the voice of a ghost writer who was just a tiny bit too late, to no
longer being afraid; here, telling you that I see you, I love you, and
that you matter. Right to the middle of you, understand the fact that
no matter what anyone else says, thinks, does or doesn't do who is
around you, this will always, always, from beyond-the-grave always,
be true. Finding **that** truth is what will show you that it's actually the
rest of the world that can Halloween-version go to straight to hell,
rather than you continuing to feel as though some inescapable living
hell has been made especially for you. You matter, right here and right
now. That is my ghost story for you. Scary stuff from your
neighborhood ghost writer, Chad. The best ghost stories that have
ever been told, are the ones telling the kept-scared parts of our souls,
of the unimaginable things that could be both un-scary, and true. Let
this one be one of those true stories for you, with me sitting here right
next to you, both of us left a little bit less scared, next to each other;
and, to ourselves at least, a little bit less scary… Now, go tell
someone else "Boo!" Hah!

<u>Blood kept warm</u>

That breathing you're doing
means that you're not
in a place to be told
By anyone
(including yourself, 'cause
even you can be a liar)
that it would be better,
for everyone if you'd stop…
Instead, living
with the understanding
that, you… here… today…
is everything.

51

the goods
—◦—♪—◦—

apart from being legally married with
my beautiful transgender woman of color,
both of us being
superheroes of the Multicolored Universe
together for eternidad
our wedding day being, to this day,
the happiest day of my life;
celebrating our 10-year anniversary
riding a bicycle built for 2
just like we did on our honeymoon,
the other,
best experience of my life so far,
was to serve
as a fulltime Mormon Missionary
at nineteen,
carrying my scriptures,

wearing
my white shirt,
tying my own non-clip-on
tie and riding
...my bicycle...
before the truth of everything,
                    detonated.

dogma
says that those two experiences
don't jibe with each other,
but that don't matter with
love

'cause the truth of what is,
no matter what dogma says,
still 'is.

<u>gonna tap that</u>

creativity is its own
elemental force of nature,
owned by no one,
wasting nothing,
breathing through each of us... freely,
not something that could ever be
stopped;
attempting to show
                    some of that breathing
                                    by
breaking sticks and pouring the blood out
onto canvas, made exquisite, like
     the words of the right poem,
  or whatever what pulsates wants
to continue
breathing through
moving
through
everyone who opens themselves up
guts to nipples

for long enough to pay attention to it
happening

        right now

    not chasing it away
      or running away from
        what it feels like when

the humid breath of elemental salvation
    moves
            towards you through you

    that - exact - feeling

        finding what has always been
involuntary, undeniable

            a life all its own
    in realtime.

guess what you don't get to do

you don't get to disappear
a whole,
flawed person's
greatness,
a group decision
made without benefit
of corrected vision,
gone down

like old bathtub water;
all of those beautiful things

that happened

are mine to remember.

I am not doing this

for money,
for attention or sensationalism for its own sake or
for myself, really, although that is certainly a part of it.
for notoriety, fuck that, in fact,
for anyone to remember me in any way, or,
in a way other than how they think they remember me.
this is not my stab at "therapy" or "a hobby"
          (fucking, really with that?)
however, there is Truth to the
satisfaction I have experienced out of the Holy
Retribution of it.
I am not trying to be relevant
to anyone
with any memorable quips
or cute-ish cleverness, I just want
Anyone
who has Ever felt
as alone as I have to know that
They are Not the only one who feels
Like this.
Whoever you are,
I fucking love you.
That is All
that all of This
is for.

102324

in case I die
before I finish writing
all of my poems
(which is likely, because obviously)
    know this: I love you.
you are of great worth
in-and-to our communal
multicolored universe
as you continue
growing
into exactly who you are;
you can do
anything,
no matter what
hateful people have to say
(as they always do, ultimately
leaving all of them unhappy anyway) so
fly and be free,
pretty please with sugar on top,
        YOU
    BEAUTIFUL HUMAN

in excelsis deo

I never get it
all the way right
with anybody,
and neither do you.
So,
occaisionally genuine
approval,
arriving in pulses nonetheless,
may feel capital-A
alright, although
it stopped mattering
as a final destination spot,
manufactured religion or not,
a long time ago.
And that
glory glory
is better than anything.

PET PEEP

Your recognition
of my gratitude,
that you've graciously expressed
by writing to me
                "your welcome"
tells me that you're giving to me
something that is already mine;
my own welcome back,
                as a matter-of-fact.
There has got to be more to what matters,
than stupid shit like
misspelled words and poor grammar
bothering me. Constantly
reminding me that
our great, shared struggle,
 as humanity,
can't even win this one, simple
gratitude boomerang fight;
 leaving me shaking my head
 in retreat, once again.
You're welcome.

Jesus is
way more rainbow
than red, white and blue,
or
plain old entitled whitey.

The politicized version of
"christianity"
is bullshit. Read the Bible
if you don't agree.

last exit

—₀—₀—₀—

nostalgia didn't make any
announcements about dying.
it just wandered out back,
arms wrapped with old
hospital wrist bands;
nodded once,
when no one was watching,

then...

lit match

—°—°—°—

they tried
to keep me from finding out
that
they're not in charge

of deciding on
who they're bringing
with them
in their carpool for Jesus.

I found out for myself
that the great big they
don't even have the right
car keys.
Buddies be
looking out for each other.
Thanks Jesus.

<u>living</u>, <u>all</u> the <u>way</u> to the <u>end</u>,
it turns out that I'm not
the person-version of a
perfectly foamed latte;
pre-positioned to consume uniformity
all in a row together
with heat-protected sleeves.
I'm not one
who was born to be
fully-formed with what is taught as
unquestionably pertinent,
its simplicity and formulas and
all of that
critical information about God and
capital H.I.S. His people,
   his fortunate few,
in a place where many are called
chosen

      to know
         that truth is completely
         intact;
         no buts.

Neither am I trying to be scary
to anyone;
faith, fear, and facts
still getting a little bit touchy
when they're too close to each   other.
I am only trying
to not be scary to me.
You used to be one of my people.
But we learned, together,
that I'm different and here's the thing:
I didn't stop living truth
when I was three, no longer needing
answers to anything
drawn from the unsafe-outside-land
     with thick pieces
          of multicolored sidewalk chalk
               on cracked pavement that
had found a way to make room
for tiny purple flowers,
like me,
who said:

"fuck you,
    get yourself safely
      back indoors.
you're blocking my sunlight and
    I'm growing here."

sheesh.
who knew
    that such a cute
      little outdoor flower

could become so bitter

and sassy.

make it a triple

how many
cross-referenced scripture
triple combinations
does it take to make the claim
of holy thought's ownership.
selected minds selectively mining
God's golden nuggets of
"double dare ya" to find
any churches other than ours
with all of
the whole truthy truth.

I love you
my marsupial dude,
curled up next to my abdomen
while I sleep.

meet me at the bayou

freedom and defeat are twins
who glide together,
undifferentiated
from each other, although never
indifferent; connected like
love's equal signs'

two lines hovering

with perfect balance, here
together
over the same body of water.

New Wings

-by Charley Gilbert

I took a drink and I floated up
Poured some more into my cup
So many drinks later, yes I could fly
But what was wrong where was the sky

I tried again the very next day
But it went wrong the very same way
Years of my failed routine, of bad flying
It never worked but I kept trying

The crashes got worse, yes down in flames
Why do I do this when it causes such pain
It's time for me to try another way
If I am to live for many more days

On my new path called sobriety
The first step in my recovery
Yes, steps not flying, take it slow
So much to learn but here I go

I asked for help, yes me the solo-flying king
Admitted I couldn't do it alone, needed a helping wing
Admitted some other things and made amends
Some tough talks with my family and friends

One day an interesting question came my way
How did you get up there and how do you stay
I looked and saw someone who looked a lot like me
So, I showed them the steps that had been shown to me

My sobriety might look like flying to them
It feels that way sometimes when I help a friend
Not always smooth with life's currents blowing
Helping is flying; are my new wings showing

<u>no more life lessons</u>

while I am asleep
my brain uses both hands
to weave fluid shapes
through magnetized mind gaps;
hungry words
entering through the front door
that sleep left unlocked again.
longing for union that no
safely shelved humans
could comprehend,
especially, those disheveled parts
where nothing really matters
and all of the fun stuff that's left
gets to fuck and flip over
and fuck again until
closing time snaps its cruel trap shut;
eyelids up again, now both
hands on ears
pulling hard
towards

daylight's serious, furrowed brows; reminders
    of how dangerous
        wanderings like
        to get lost like that

mean as fuck
gravity holding me here
without my permission when I am

wishing to be swimming
through
        rain-slicked
        road
        surfaces'
        false barriers
lovehumping everything
I can see again.

open to air

when is the wound that is left
way over there,
 inna gonna scar-ya
 for all of the life that is;
left with the thoughtless
biomechanics of healing,
sharing the same space with you as
the open air of not wanting to think
about any of it,
Caught-up in a tango dance of not able
        not gonna and
cannot won't   look directly
 at your heart's open wound when you
didn't see it
coming right at you
lying in a lying casket
lid wide opened
ready-prepped with a smile
for you to can't with your own eyes
Your best friend from the first day
that you met. It isn't time for
anything but this is not happening.

Recycle Day
(a joyful, hopeful poem)

Even the good stuff piles up in corners,
sometimes.
forget about the stuff that you just can't
make yourself
throw out on recycle day... and forget...
decades, left in stacks...
                         with all of that...
potential
for clinical paralysis;
prioritization creating its tangled lists
then
threatening you with toppling
everything over.
burying you alive
if you're leering
too much or too little,
just tiptoe through
those neighborhoods of precarious

leaning towers,
you know exactly what I mean.
Just like seeing
that same goddamn meal
you never even ordered,
showing up at your front door
and ringing the bell like a boss
with a big bag of to-go
dont-go-there drunken noodles;
growth
choking you with its chopsticks
pinching chunky words
that
won't
toggle
all the way down
or come back up,
like roadblocks
smothered in hot sauce
headed for the wrong pipe
and here we are;
crying through every meal again.

you don't ever look in a mirror
when you already know
what you won't see
looking backwards.,
          poor Mister Macho,
all the way lost while still not
presently wanting
to ask for directions
from a therapist. Just go ahead.
We can call it recycle day.

                    for Tzvi

the shadow I have

is here to defend me, or
something; usually content enough
to stick around behind me,
passive about watching each day
unfolding on its wavy conveyor belt,
      here, and along for the ride,
matching each situation, with tricks
of shifting light, usually sneaking by,
quietly, without hiding behind me,
waking a deeper something now,
within my shadow pal, standing
all stretched out in front of me into
nearly blind darkness
            no matter the path.
hands kept casual to their sides, he
fills the frames of closed doors; quietly
      opening them for me,
            why, thank you, and
either behaving or misbehaving like
   an unannounced gentleman.

forever Shadrach

riding free with me
the wind dancing
between and around us, three as one
and with me
forgiven for losing him,
the way that I did.
that part is over and it is just
us, together again,
riding everywhere with no helmet and
zero clothing on again
     ...'cause...that truly was...
fantastic as fuck.
spur of the moment roadtrip, ready,
him and me
with or without
enough gas or any plan just
going.
flashing lights and sounds
of ambulance sirens
never catching up
with us...here together
     ...for...fucking...ever...

Shoreline
—o—o—o—

Once upon a time, I was afraid
to come up out of the water
because I didn't have any legs and
I was born to be all slimy and stuff, not
up on some dirt hill to dry out
like a hungry seagull's potato chip.
This watery spot is still comfy-home;
and... and... the right time...
to crawl out...
wasn't quite yet...
until I saw
this one guy,
named
John Motherfucking Kirby Motherfuckers;
born to spend his life pulling
people's heads
outta their asses,
especially when they'd gotten themselves
all fuckered.
Walking up and down the same shoreline
where I remained water logged,

less happy watching him
somehow having some kind of
upright hinge-legs
and feet taking him everywhere,
to look at everything
that needed to happen next
as I attempted to remain hidden,
blinking at him as quietly as I could
when...
direct eye contact! shit! he saw me!
now my head is gonna get yanked outta my butt!
but, somehow nah, he didn't do that.
he just kept on walking and
being a badass as I watched and watched
those hinge-legs and feet
walking; the way that he somehow
automatically knew
to be doing exactly what he was doing,
when I figured out
that I kinda wanted to be a badass too,
and began, slowly crawling
up outta the water, after...
being completely sure...
that there weren't
any hungry seagulls flying around.

slomo homo

you know
how lucky you are
to still be catching
anything;
that door frame, barely in time,
getting lucky
today is... an aging elbow...
that won't let you fall down,
not hearing
"just stand here"
from anyone, yet somehow
not hurrying to leave; just
remembering that important fact:
one place for one moment of
catching your breath;
this darkened closet...
lights flipped on again.
repurposed;
all of that useless clothing
removed and
replaced with not quite yet
uselessness, now only

here for listening
for what you used to hear,
leaning with
the doorway and
holding hands with
         an absentminded
hairbrush.
photographs affixed
to this stillness among
four narrow walls that know, they
don't have to say anything
for you to hear everything,
unblinking eyes looking at you
from wherever they
didn't die, we are all still here;
not so suddenly, gone all
   grown-older together, unjudging
         eyes loving watching
            you not fall too soon
as you brush your purple hair
in slow motion.

sperm of the moment

I'm most likely not
gonna be very happy about this
later, in fact, I will
most likely, immediately
become extremely depressed,
hoping that nobody I know
can see what's written on my face,
maybe not
exactly where I've been
but, clearly,
that I have been somewhere where
I shouldn't have been, doing things,
maybe with someone, or more than one
who, I cannot talk about but that,
my face, especially my cheeks and
one hundred percent yes,
my eyes won't shut up about it;
hoping that nobody will be at home,
at least for a little while,
when I get there so that I'll have
a chance...

to scrub that

    look off of my face, and

practice my nothing happened,
while just walking around with

my best friend, Normalcy,

    Singing songs about forgiveness,
to JESUS and GOD

until anybody gets home,

without crying the whole time

about going to hell for sure,

this time.

one more time

Sometimes, you don't know
the time that you're having together
is going to be the last time and
Sometimes, you do know.
both of you know
at the same time that you both
    know to savor
    that moment while you are both
                inside of that same moment
happening spontaneously horizontal once more
    on the hallway floor with
        one quick pull-down to get
shorts and boxers completely off and thrown
    somewhere before we overthink
    two   t-shirts chasing them,
bare arms wrapped around bare backs
 up to each other's arm pits; bare chest
          pressed   into   bare chest
heads nuzzled together - each - other's
    ...perfectly...fitted...temples...
the way that only we two
have ever been able to
tuck into the contours of
pi.
no need to ask each other why. here,
eleven years out from our first overnight
waking up the following morning,
still holding hands from the night before.

spunk
_|.—.—.._—
from another's gear
ain't gonna
get to
skip out of
finding itself
smudging
around here
in
my
book.

to saltlick

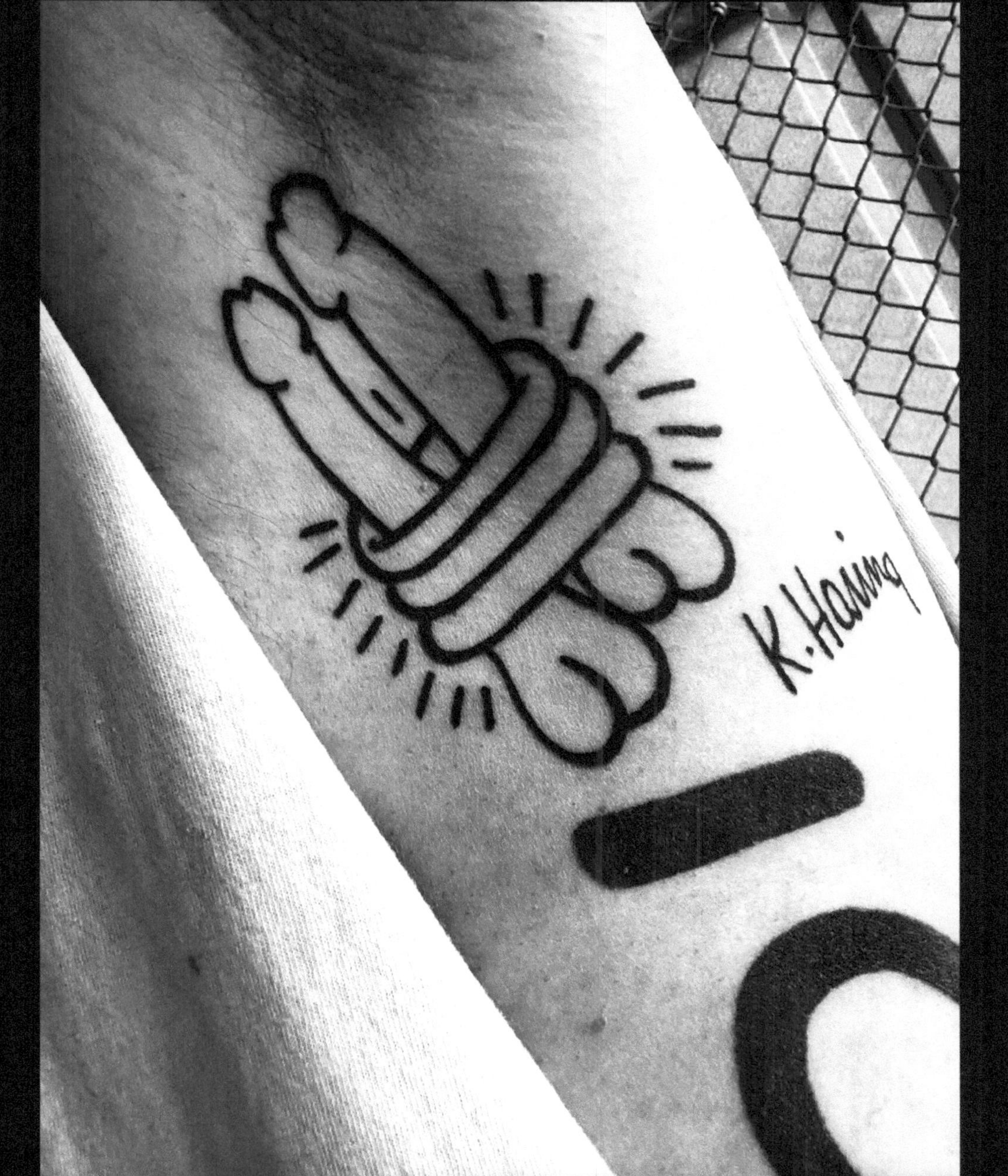
K.Haring

(3×+) three of 3v37y+ding

Maybe it starts
with an unimagined third eye awakening,
or maybe nothing ever begins when
all of this was already happening;
the same reverberations of trees
growing in rooted directions, within whether
or not anyone is present
to listen to their omnipresent music.
this is the opening moment
your very own grove, correlating
with your very own groove and you,
collaborating;
finding your mind shifting
into space-math's next non-conforming
complexity, its rhythms
measuring with toe-taps
the three of everything.
At least that is where and when
my own grove of trees tutored me.
I will see you there, here,
or wherever else, glittering
with that unmistakably sweet
soul deep clarity; this sweat is
for you... to continue...

Today is this...

listening to a song
for the first time that feels
like it was lifted
directly from my head.

watching a fully grown deer
standing on her hind legs
reaching the leaves of high branches.

tasting sparkles
through cool water; my body
thanking me.

The presence of life's best ever
companionship;
their olfactory-driven directions
merging with treats, then,

the deeply satisfying scent
of weightlessness
found in the space between
their temples and furry ears.

My tattooed left hand holding
my favorite pen, my tattooed
right hand holding a blank page
finding balance
between gravity and blast-off
with long, purple hair and ink
registering
time
and velocity

                        and stopping

for long enough
to watch clouds moving by.

It can become
a whole lotta fun
when you don't fit
the way that they
want you to fit
especially
if they ever
try to insist.

You,
laughing

"HAH!"

is the cherry on top.

what happens today

after so much political bullshit
  went the wrong way
again, is the same thing
that happened
yesterday and the day before yesterday and
last year and the year before last year
and ten years from now; then
twenty, just like
what happened when I was growing up
before I knew better;
before I found out that
people who I don't know... or did,
would hate
my people
and me
without any of us understanding why.
I am the same person
now, then, and all of the tomorrows,
not really mattering
to any of the haters, and them,
not mattering to me.
My people and I have discovered how

to carry ourselves and each other through
    all of this life
with our beautiful, perennial love,
    no matter what.
And that, motherfuckers,
    will never motherfucking stop.

I will look any smug-ass piece of shit
in both eyes without blinking, and with
both feet firmly planted on the ground,
will make certain that they understand
I am living here.

11624

<u>ya wanna know</u>

what pisses me off is people
who don't know anything
about my beautiful;
telling me that I am doing my thing
the wrong way for them, and then,
when I continue to feel ALL of the
fullness of my life's beautiful journey,
anyway,
having to put up a fight,
which I will,
leaving them nothing but piled up pulp
and heaving; sidewalk residue.
it is unwise to determine
        =that they have any right=
to undermine the beauty of what
        ...I feel and see...
yanking my love away from me
"for my own good."
only one of us survives
the soul-fascism you're talking about.
now it's your turn to be taught
what to do about people like me.

remember the time

I still have the pen that you gave to me,
sitting next to your picture from 30 years ago
although, I can't remember the pen
ever working, proving to me that
it communicated its intended message
effectively, working or not working and
not wrapped in anything
when you gave it to me with only
a thin string attached to its clip;
tiny, the white slip of paper
tied to the other end
with a handwritten command...write!
it sucks that you were not able to
get to the end of this lifespan with me.
you, not here, not getting to say
"Remember that time" with me now;
then, remembering you saying
"I remember, all of this, here today
with the heartbeats from each of your
handwritten poems, like this one,
to me; since, happening, at all, lives forever."

a stranger's respects

I am not going to Louisiana
for anyone's funeral
that I know.
It's someone else's
hole that has been dug into the ground

that I'll be standing next to,
with
       my head bowed,

crying
for

   someone

who I don't know
who left

         before I got to go;

breathing gone homeless

  once more.

name that sonic boom

just because
the rhythm is
a complicated one
doesn't mean that you haven't found it
shuddering and stillness are
negotiating
shifting balances and instinctively
competing interests
just keep on dancing
your motherfucking ass off,
      'cause Girl
You Lookin' Good.

while

today being today
—o—o—o—

as if it had any choice
in the matter
or in what matters for today.
it only gets one of these.
this one.
counting down for it
like a kid at christmas or
a prisoner reaching parole day.
it's finally getting its one chance
in all of the universe of time
to be presented
to the whole world
right through the front door:
"presenting Today"
for a limited engagement
before joining the bajillions
of previous days to be baked
into was-ism cakes,

but, before any of that;

see...

this is today's one chance

→ to be ... what is ←

...

...shapes...blossom...here...

...Mom, spending a month sewing homemade matching bathrobes for all of my brothers and me, one Christmas; her sewing machine, in its permanent spot along the wall next to our family's dining table...

...Stephen, living in the apartment right next door during our mutual thirties, providing reliable friendship, delicious homemade dinners, playing Kate Bush and Tori Amos while giving me a listening ear when I couldn't stop talking about this new guy I was dating named Drew...

…one queer human named Mason, superhero-level brave in a small town red state, bringing together over two hundred local LGBTQ+ humans and genuine allies, each one previously feeling more like a local total anomaly, better left hidden, now feeling true community, openly, for the very first time, right here in our own little town…

… now, just like with my books that came before this one, here are a few pages for you to WRITE the SHAPES of your own LIFE making blossoms…

… on your mark, get set,

grow